Family Storybook Library

The Humblest Package Can Contain the Greatest Gift

Stories About Fairness and Judgment

BOOK NINE

First Edition
1 3 5 7 9 10 8 6 4 2

ISBN: 0-7868-5874-5

The Humblest Package Can Contain the Greatest Gift

———✧✧✧———

Stories About Fairness and Judgment

Introduction

The old adage states, "Children must be taught to hate." It's true that while children certainly notice and often point out differences between people, they don't automatically attribute undesirable characteristics to those who differ from themselves. That's an ugly quality that they learn from those around them as they grow older. This prejudice should be actively discouraged— for everyone has something to offer; something unique to teach us. Each person has an innate dignity, which should be cultivated and celebrated.

Although the townspeople despise Quasimodo, he doesn't let that stop him from saving Esmeralda's life. While not everyone loves Lady as much as her family does, her quick thinking and bravery save the life of a tiny baby.

Quasimodo's Quick Thinking

from *The Hunchback of Notre Dame*

The humblest packages can contain the greatest gifts.

Igh above the city streets, Quasimodo watched the scene from the cathedral. Frollo, the wicked Minister of Justice, had sentenced the beautiful gypsy, Esmeralda, to death. Quasimodo knew that Frollo was capable of terrible things. After all, it had been Frollo who had banished the poor hunchbacked bell ringer to a life isolated from other people. Now Quasimodo feared for Esmeralda's life. He had to save her, but how? Frollo had locked him high in the cathedral bell tower.

The shouts of the crowd below grew louder and louder. Quasimodo paced anxiously back and forth, not sure what to do. Time was running out for Esmeralda. Quasimodo brushed past one of the heavy ropes for the bells and suddenly had an idea.

Quasimodo tied one end of a rope to a heavy gargoyle perched on the edge of the roof. Then, with a mighty shout, he leaped off, holding the other end of the rope. The wind whistled in his ears as he swooped down like an eagle. The rope swung right over Esmeralda. Quasimodo reached out and grabbed his friend, pulling her to safety.

"Get them!" shouted Frollo. He was furious that the hunchback had foiled his plans.

Quasimodo and
Esmeralda escaped
to the cathedral
with Frollo's soldiers
close behind. Soon the
cathedral was
surrounded, but
Quasimodo was
not ready to give up.

"Quick, this way!"
he called to Esmeralda.
They hurried to the
bell tower. A huge
pot of hot, liquid
lead bubbled there.
Quasimodo used the
lead to repair cracks
in the bells, but today

it would serve a different purpose.
Together, Quasimodo and
Esmeralda lifted the pot to
a spot right above the
soldiers. Hot steam
rose into the air.
With a nod to each
other, they tilted
the pot so that the
hot lead poured
out, down to where
the soldiers were
battering down the
door.
"NO!" cried Frollo
in frustration as the soldiers
dashed away from the boiling
lead. His troops retreated as the crowd

cheered for Quasimodo's quick thinking.

Quasimodo and Esmeralda looked down and heaved a sigh of relief. They were safe from Frollo and his men, thanks to Quasimodo, the hunchback of Notre Dame.

Lady to the Rescue

from *Lady and the Tramp*

Everyone deserves a chance to explain.

L ady was a very sad dog. Her owners had gone away, leaving Aunt Sarah to care for her and the baby until they returned. Taking care of the baby was a joy for Aunt Sarah. But she had no time for dogs. Poor Lady was chained in the yard, wishing Jim Dear and Darling would come home soon. To make matters worse, it was starting to rain.

Suddenly Lady sat up. Something was moving toward the house.

"Arf! Arf Arf!" Lady barked.

"Be quiet!" shouted Aunt Sarah.

Then, in the moonlight, Lady could see a rat creeping up a vine to the baby's room!

"Hey, Pigeon," called a friendly voice. It was Lady's friend Tramp.

"Help!" Lady barked. "A rat is in the baby's room!"

Tramp wasted no time. He rushed in a back door and dashed upstairs. The rat was already scurrying toward the cradle.

Lady heard Tramp and the rat fighting. She tugged with all her might and pulled free of the chain. Barking loudly, Lady ran into the house.

Aunt Sarah

heard the commotion in the nursery and
ran to see what was the matter. The baby
was crying and the room was a mess.

"Oh! Oh! You dreadful dogs!" she cried. "Oh, the poor baby!" She thought Lady and Tramp had tried to hurt the child.

There was no way for Lady to explain. Aunt Sarah locked Tramp in a closet and called the dogcatcher. Then she tied Lady up outside again.

"Imagine, trying to hurt a helpless little baby!" she said. "You should be ashamed!"

Just then, Lady heard Jim Dear and Darling return home. She barked and barked until they let her loose. Then she dashed back to the nursery with them close behind.

"Keep those vicious dogs away from the baby!" Aunt Sarah screamed. "They're jealous of him!"

Lady paid no attention to Aunt Sarah. She ran to a tangled curtain and barked until Jim Dear unrolled it.

"A rat!" exclaimed Darling. "Why, that's why the dogs were in here! They saved the baby!"

Lady was very glad the baby was safe. Jim Dear and Darling asked the brave Tramp to live with them always, and he was happy to agree.

As for Aunt Sarah, she realized that dogs weren't so bad after all, and sent them a tin of dog biscuits every Christmas!